Albie
the
Lifeguard

by Louise Borden

Illustrated by Elizabeth Sayles

For Will, who makes a big 'SPLASH!

Elizabeth Sayles

SCHOLASTIC INC.

New York Toronto London Auckland Sydney
Mexico City New Delhi Hong Kong

For Cindy and Marg,
oldest swimming friends
—L.B.

To Uncle Seymour
—E.S.

Special thanks to Jackie,
who gave me the title...
and to M.K.,
who was an Albie,
years ago.

ISBN 0-590-44586-3

Text copyright © 1993 by Louise Borden.
Illustrations copyright © 1993 by Elizabeth Sayles.
All rights reserved.
Published by Scholastic Inc.
SCHOLASTIC and associated logos are trademarks and/or registered trademarks of Scholastic Inc.

12 11 10 9 8 7 6 5 4 3   9/9 0 1 2 3/0

Printed in the U.S.A.   14

First Scholastic paperback printing, July 1993

The illustrations in this book were done with pastel.

The day the town pool opened for the summer,
Ward, Will, Em, and Tony
all signed up for the Dolphin swim team.
Right away. First thing.
They wrote their names at the top of the list.

DEEP

7FT

But not Albie.
Albie hitched up his suit and carefully read the swim team categories posted on the pool bulletin board:

Team Practice
9am SHARP!
Freestyle, backstroke, breaststroke, butterfly.

Albie looked at the lap lanes, long and blue.
He couldn't swim a whole length of the pool without stopping... not in a *race*!

Instead, Albie did a cannonball
off the board and made
a *huge splash*!

He dove for pennies, gleaming copper
on the bottom of the pool.

He leaped into the deep end
with a karate shriek
and then bobbed about like a slippery seal.

Then he sat underwater in the shallow end
and had a tea party with his two big sisters.

Albie knew how to have a good time at the town pool.

While he waited for his buddies,
Albie watched the lifeguards sitting in
their tall chairs, swinging their whistles,
cleaning their sunglasses, and calling out
important instructions:

"SLOW DOWN!"
"NO RUNNING!"
"NO DUNKING!"
and **"NO FOOD NEAR THE POOL!"**

That's when Albie decided to play lifeguard...
in his own backyard.

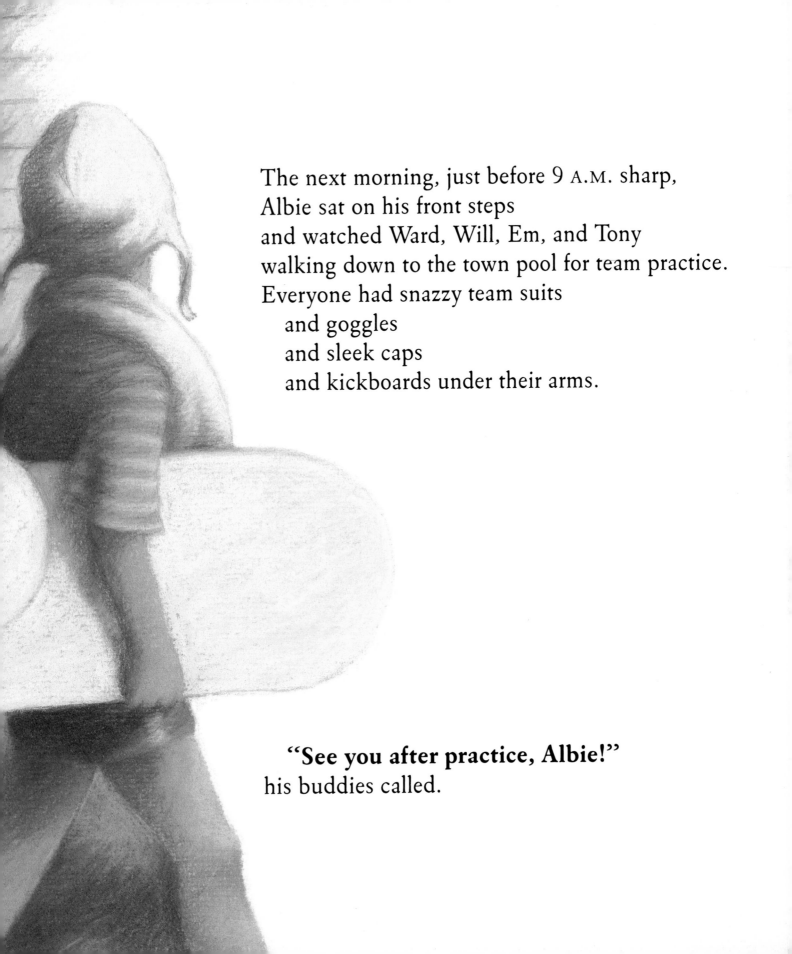

The next morning, just before 9 A.M. sharp,
Albie sat on his front steps
and watched Ward, Will, Em, and Tony
walking down to the town pool for team practice.
Everyone had snazzy team suits
    and goggles
    and sleek caps
    and kickboards under their arms.

"See you after practice, Albie!"
his buddies called.

Albie hurried into his house and
climbed the stairs to his attic.
There,
    in the dustiest corner,
    covered with cobwebs,
    was his guard chair.
It was just the right size
and even had some rungs to climb.

Albie put on his jazziest bathing suit,
his sister's sunglasses,
wrapped a beach towel around his waist,
and headed for his backyard.

All morning,
Albie sat high in his guard chair,
swinging his whistle around his finger.

Albie shifted in his chair
and listened to his neighbor, Mrs. Salerno,
playing the piano.
Albie could tell she was just a beginner.

Then he blew his whistle loudly and announced:

**"WILL EVERYONE UNDER THE AGE
OF 18 PLEASE CLEAR THE POOL?
IT IS NOW TIME FOR ADULT SWIM!"**

There were many things for a backyard lifeguard to do:
    like setting up umbrellas on sunny days
    and listening for thunder on cloudy days
    and, of course,
    making sure there were *no diapers* in the big pool.

Albie saved a toddler who tripped over a kickboard and tumbled into the deep end.

Then he broke up a water balloon fight between some smart alecks who were playing rough.

And then he had to throw the life ring from the back of his chair to save a grandmother who got a leg cramp in the lap lane.

Things were so busy that Albie helped out
in the snack bar when his shift was over.
The Blue Rocket ice cream bars sold out fast.

Albie looked at his waterproof watch.
Swim team practice was almost over,
so he closed his backyard pool for the day.
Albie left his whistle and his sunglasses
and his life ring down by the deep end,
right by his chair. He hopped on his bike
and pedaled to the town pool,
humming summer songs all the way.

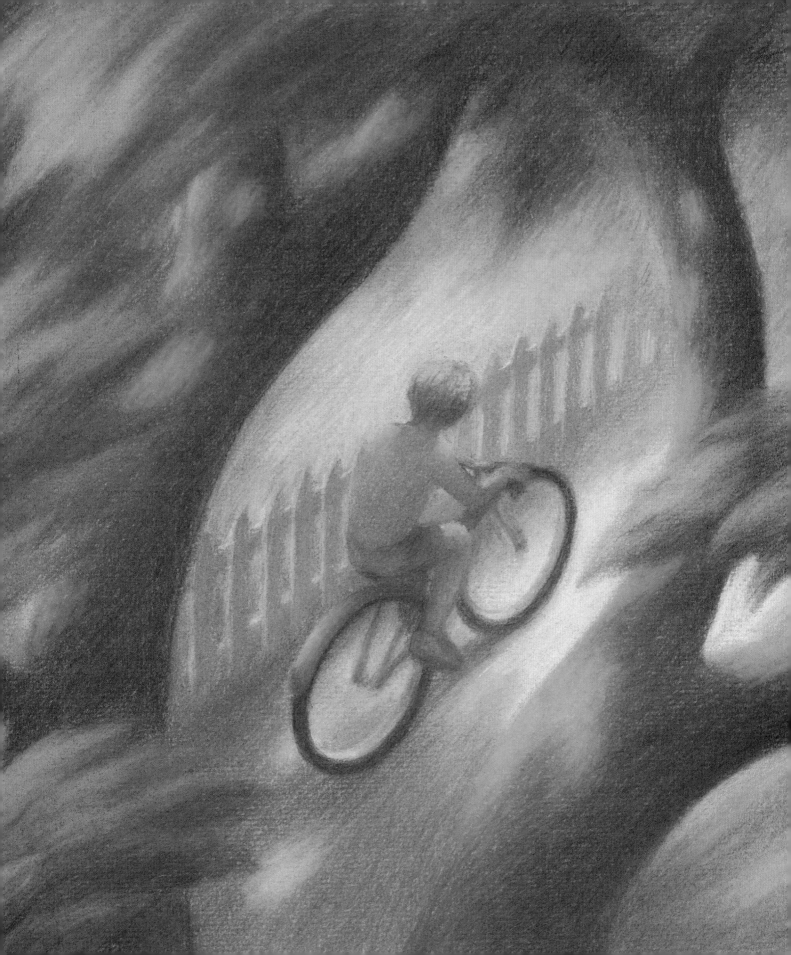

There were his buddies,
waiting for Albie,
in their wet team caps
and wet team suits.

Albie showed Ward how to make
a bigger splash with his cannonball.
He shared his shiniest pennies with Will.
And later,
Albie had an underwater party
with Em and Tony,
and let his guests pour the tea.

Albie knew how to have a good time
at the town pool.

On the day of the first swim meet,
Albie helped the pool manager hang a string
of flags across the pool for the Dolphins.
And then Albie stayed to watch his buddies on the team.
  He cheered the loudest
  and clapped the longest
  even though they lost.
Even though Tony didn't swim the whole length of the pool.

"But that's okay," said Albie.
"You'll do it next time."
And he patted Ward and Will and Em and Tony on the back.
In June, the Dolphins lost more than they won.
Albie went to every meet.

On the Fourth of July,
Albie stood for a long time
by the guard chair,
looking at the length of the pool.
The lap lanes seemed a little shorter.
And so he wrote his name in bold, black pencil
at the bottom of the swim team sign-up list.

At the next practice,
Albie showed up in a snazzy team suit
    and goggles
    and a sleek cap
    and carried a kickboard under his arm.

Ward helped him with the breaststroke.
He butterflied right behind Will.
And Em and Tony said Albie was terrific at
backstroke and freestyle.

On all the mornings after that,
when the town pool shone like a blue mirror,
Albie arrived at practice before
the rest of the Dolphin swim team.
And for a few minutes,
Albie had the town pool all to himself.